Messy Dogs

Dona Herweck Rice

Library of Congress Cataloging-in-Publication Data

Names: Rice, Dona, author.
Title: Messy dogs / Dona Herweck Rice.
Description: Huntington Beach, CA : Teacher Created Materials, [2019] | Audience: Age 4-6. |
Identifiers: LCCN 2018020223 (print) | LCCN 2018021388 (ebook) | ISBN 9781493898916 () | ISBN 9781493898176 (paperback)
Subjects: LCSH: Dogs--Juvenile literature.
Classification: LCC SF426.5 (ebook) | LCC SF426.5 .R525 2019 (print) | DDC 636.7--dc23
LC record available at https://lccn.loc.gov/2018020223

Publishing Credits

Rachelle Cracchiolo, M.S.Ed., *Publisher*
Conni Medina, M.A.Ed., *Managing Editor*
Nika Fabienke, Ed.D., *Content Director*
Véronique Bos, *Creative Director*
Shaun N. Bernadou, *Art Director*
Carol Huey-Gatewood, M.A.Ed., *Editor*
Valerie Morales, *Associate Editor*
Courtney Roberson, *Senior Graphic Designer*

Image Credits: All images from iStock and/or Shutterstock.

Teacher Created Materials
5301 Oceanus Drive
Huntington Beach, CA 92649-1030
www.tcmpub.com

ISBN 978-1-4938-9817-6
© 2019 Teacher Created Materials, Inc.
Printed by: 590835
Printed in: Taiwan

They are in  .

mud

They are in  .

trash

They are in  .

shoes

They are in  .

clothes

They are in  .

leaves

They are in  .

snow

They are in  .

sand

They are in  .

water

They are in  .

families

They are in ❤ .

love

High-Frequency Words

are

in

they